W9-AYX-163

PRAISE FOR *DARK TESTAMENT*

"I love this tremendously skillful, timely, and dazzling repurposing of passages of my novel *Lincoln in the Bardo*. Crystal Simone Smith has, with her amazing ear and heart, found, in that earlier grief, a beautiful echo for our time."

—George Saunders, *New York Times*–bestselling author of *Lincoln in the Bardo* and *Tenth of December*

"How profoundly fitting that these elegies for lost sons and daughters be structured as subtractive blackout poems. Crystal Smith has created a collection not only reflective of our grief but worthy of our loss."

—Carole Boston Weatherford, Coretta Scott King Award winner for *Unspeakable: The Tulsa Race Massacre*

"Crystal Simone Smith is one of the most vibrant, clear-eyed, and gifted poets writing today, and *Dark Testament* could not be a more necessary or important response to the fractured world in which we find ourselves. Smith shines a light and raises her bright voice, one that connects history to the present—timelessness and timeliness—and gives us the gift of remembering these harrowing losses, these beautiful lives. She testifies, and I can't wait to hear a chorus of amens sung in response."

—Haven Kimmel, #1 *New York Times*–bestselling author of *A Girl Named Zippy*, *Orville: A Dog Story*, and *Kaline Klattermaster's Tree House*

"From the wellspring of a fictional text on Abraham Lincoln, poet Crystal Simone Smith emancipates words, phrases, and snatched-up lines to celebrate the tragic lives of those enslaved by racism, stupidity, and the brutal reality of the system of American policing that can be to Black and Brown alike a Dante's hell. These trigger(ed)-collages, excavated from an existing text, teach us that language, like breathing, belongs to everyone, and its elasticity is as resilient and tenuous as Blackness and being. *Dark Testament* is a multilayered, symphonic meditation-conversation breathing life into what we witness and must remember. What Smith carves from these black-and-white found erasures etches its way into the (un)conscious/conscience of a nascent nation still grappling with its original sin."

—Tony Medina, poet and author of *I Am Alfonso Jones* and *Thirteen Ways of Looking at a Black Boy*

"It has never been the case that death has no voice. And these poems, by Crystal Simone Smith, remind us of this—making the case not just that the memories of Trayvon Martin, Freddie Gray, and Oscar Grant matter, but that what they might say of the world is always far more nuanced and complicated than we might imagine. What Smith has been able to do with these poems is compelling."

—Reginald Dwayne Betts, lawyer and poet, author of *A Question of Freedom: A Memoir of Learning, Survival, and Coming of Age in Prison* and *Felon*

DARK TESTAMENT

POEMS

CRYSTAL SIMONE SMITH

HENRY HOLT AND COMPANY

NEW YORK

Henry Holt and Company, *Publishers since 1866*
Henry Holt® is a registered trademark of Macmillan Publishing Group, LLC
120 Broadway, New York, NY 10271 • fiercereads.com

Text copyright © 2023 by Crystal Simone Smith
Photographs and artwork copyright © 2023 as detailed on pages 53–84.
All rights reserved.

Our books may be purchased in bulk for promotional, educational, or
business use. Please contact your local bookseller or the Macmillan Corporate
and Premium Sales Department at (800) 221–7945 ext. 5442 or by email at
MacmillanSpecialMarkets@macmillan.com.

Library of Congress Control Number: 2022916283

First edition, 2023
Book design by Aurora Parlagreco
Printed in the United States of America

ISBN 978-1-250-85436-0
10 9 8 7 6 5 4 3 2 1

for Black mothers and sons everywhere

PART ONE

INTRODUCTION

When deaths occur, we are tasked with celebrating while we mourn. *Dark Testament* transports us to that gracious yet daunting place. It is a tribute to Black lives lost in our often *dark* world, and a *testament* to the fragility of our world, one where we struggle, with great vigor, to coexist as humans. We are aware of this struggle most when we encounter violence. We are assigned complex labels—unarmed, vigilante, witness, suspect, victim—that distract us from the fact that America is a nation uncured of racism, one that still asks us to condone hatred and bias as part of its culture. We are tasked with accepting the worst we can do to one another.

Dark Testament was written in response to the recorded police killing of George Floyd. After the footage's release, the nation swelled into a wave of rage and civil unrest, eclipsing even the pandemic ravaging the country. While watching protestors amass for days calling for the arrest of the officers, I was reading *Lincoln in the Bardo* as research for a novel I was writing. The nation was also reeling from the recent murder of jogger Ahmaud Arbery.

As the mother of two Black sons, I found the agony

crushing, and I struggled to navigate it. My teenager, a distance runner like Arbery, had transformed into a towering figure, mellow-spirited yet fully vulnerable to police encounters. I had reached a personal tipping point. The depth of this nation's fixation with race was starkly apparent to me— a Black body meant a target, with the goal of elimination.

George Saunders's *Lincoln in the Bardo* is an extraordinary, experimental novel, wrought with anguish, that centers on the grief Lincoln endures after the death of his eleven-year-old son, Willie. As I continued reading Saunders's book, certain words and phrases began to loom in the text, eerily articulating the despair I held. I felt compelled to explore these ghostly voices calling to me, and what emerged was a collection of blackout poems.

Thus, the process of eliminating words to create blackout poems was not accidental. It was a very conscious decision— almost instinctual—as the well-being of my sons, the one thing most central to my thinking and living, felt endangered.

Indeed, all lives include death. However, in reading *Dark Testament*, we can consider in meaningful and profound ways the lives of these victims: Oscar Grant, the doting father; Tamir Rice, the lanky, lovable son; and Breonna Taylor, the decorated first responder. As a statement of fact, I say "victims," but all these people were equally treasured beings who left families and communities tasked with living in a world without them. As the poet, I task you the reader with lighting a conscience flame in honor of those killed by violence, and carrying that torch into a more just future.

A better world is within our grasp.

A NOTE TO THE READER

Dark Testament is an interactive text. Each poem is a visual created literally using the written word. The blank pages within represent a pause of remembrance. They are meant to be experienced. Silence is often an act in which those still living undertake to be worthy of those who died.

PART ONE

NO JUSTICE, NO PEACE

███████████ If such things as goodness and brotherhood and redemption exist, and may be attained, these must ██████████ require █████████████████████████ ████████████████████████████ the vanquishing of the heartless oppressor. ████████████████████████████

██████████████████

████████████████████████████████

We are dead, I said.

████████████████████████

██████ no more—████████████████████

█████████

████████████████████████████

██████████ I said ████████

███████████████████████████████████████

███████████████

████████████████████

OSCAR GRANT

Please ███████ understand. We had been ██████ fathers. Had been ████████████████ men █████ ████████████████████████████████ ███████ sorrowful ███ surging forward ██████ █████████ damaged ████████████ Had been young ██████████████████ our gentle qualities stripped from us by ████████████ circumstance, ████████████████████████ ██████████████████████████████ ██████████████████████████████ ██████████ men, ████████████ who, █████ █████ had come to grasp our ████████████ ████████████████████████ heavy burden), ████████████████ if we would not be *great*, we would be *useful*; ████████████████ thereby able to effect good: smiling, hands in pockets, watching the world ██████████████████████████████ ██████████████████████████████ ████████████████████████ ███ cheering █████████████████████████ on days ████████████████████ tolerant ███

of   dark secrets

What I mean to say is, we had

been loved. Not lonely, not lost,

not freakish,

loved

loved, I say

ERIC GARNER

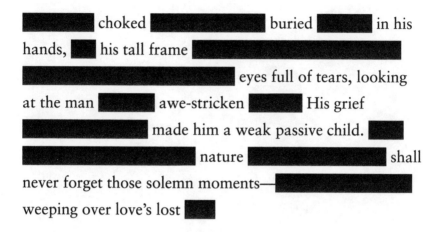

███████ choked ████████████ buried █████ in his
hands, ██ his tall frame ███████████████████
████████████████████ eyes full of tears, looking
at the man ███████ awe-stricken ███████ His grief
███████████████ made him a weak passive child. ███
███████████████████████ nature ████████████ shall
never forget those solemn moments—████████████████
weeping over love's lost █████

BLACK MOTHERS AND SONS

I am waiting to be discovered ███████████████
████ head ████████████ upended ████████████████
██
████████████████ the awful mess ██████████ (Mother
will not be pleased), ████████████████████████
██
████████████████████████████████████ Having
come so close to losing everything, ████████████
██
devoutly ██████████████████████████████████
loving █████████████████████████ standing very
still among the beautiful things of this world, ██████
█████████████████ dream-kicking ██████████
██
rearranged ████████████████████████████████
passing ship-like ████████████████████████████
██ while
██████████ in town, a purple-blue day unfolds ███████
███████████████████ each moist-grassed, flower-pierced
yard gone positively mad ██████

11

TRAYVON MARTIN

It was real.
   As real as the trees now swaying above me ████████
████████████████████ as real as the fading, ████████
breathing shallowly ████████████████████████████
██ chest ████ captive ██████████████ victim of ██
negligence ████████████████████████████
██████████████████████ as real as Mr. ████████████
████ who ████ came run-skimming up the path, looking
████████████████████████████████ seen ████
██████████████████████████████████
████████████████████
██████████████████████████████████
██████████████████████████████████
██████
██████████████████████████████
██████████
████ He entered the clearing ████████ us, holding a lock:
██ lock to the door of
████████████████████████
grief ████████████████████████████████
   The moon shone down brightly ████████████████
████████████
████████████████

SYBRINA FULTON

We have loved each other well, ████████████████ for
reasons we cannot understand, that bond has been broken.
But ██████ can never be broken. As long as I live, ███
████████████████████████
████████████████

████████████████████████████ no matter
████████████████████████████████

████████████████ Please know ████████ that you
were a joy. ████ Every minute, every season, you ████████
did a good job ████████ of being a pleasure to know.

████████████████████████████████
████████████████████████████████████
████████████████████████████████████
████████████████████████████████

████████████ I ██ now ████████████
████████ know exactly what he was
████████ the way his long legs lay ████████████
████████

████████████████████████████████
████████████

the feel of him in my arms ████████████████████

██████████████

███████████████████████████

███████████████████

██████████████████████████

████████████████████████████

██████████████████████ him still, ████████

████████████████ the heft of him familiar from when he

would fall asleep █████████ and I would carry him ██████

████████████

████████████

█████████████████████████████████ up;

████████████

████████████ I shall do my duty in other

matters; █████████

██████████████████████████

████████████ I shall take away from here

this resolve: ██████████████████████

█████████████████████████████

no more.

███████████████

Dear boy, ███████████████ That is a promise.

#BLM

███████ we must, we felt, do all we could, in light of the
many ████████ dead ██████████████████████████
█ across the land, █████████████████████████
███████████████████████████████████████
███████████████████████████████████████
██████████████████████████ as we trod that difficult
path █████ now well upon, ███████████████████
███████████████████████████████████████
█████ more ██████ boys, each of whom was once dear to
someone.

███████████████████ we ████ must endeavor ████████
████████████

Our grief ████████████████ must ████████████████████
██████████████████████ put us even deeper in ████████
████

MICHAEL BROWN

The dead lay ███████ fallen, ████████████████

some grasping their guns ████████████████

███████ while others, ████████████ in their █ grasp

██ wore

a ████████████████████████████████ fiendish

look of hate. It looked as though ██████████████

██

████████████████████ the death messenger laid ██ low.

████████ noble-looking youth, with his ████████

turned face, with his glossy ████████████████

life-blood, ██████████████████████████

as his young life went out. ████████████████

████ a prayer ████████████ little one ████████ on his

lips. Youth and age, virtue and evil, ██████████████

██████████████████████ Before us lay the ████████

████████████ remains of some who had been ████ alive. ████

██

consumed ████

JORDAN DAVIS

When a child is lost there is no end to the ▮ torment ▮
▮▮▮▮▮

▮▮▮▮ When we love, and the object of our love is
▮▮▮▮▮

▮▮ vulnerable, and has ▮▮▮▮▮▮▮ us alone for
protection;

▮▮▮▮▮▮▮▮▮▮▮▮▮▮▮▮▮▮

▮▮▮ what consolation
(what justification, ▮▮▮▮▮▮ may there possibly be?
None.

▮▮▮▮▮▮▮▮▮▮▮

▮▮▮▮▮ one occasion ▮▮▮▮▮▮▮ addressed,
another and then another ▮▮ arise in its place.

THE WORLD AND ME

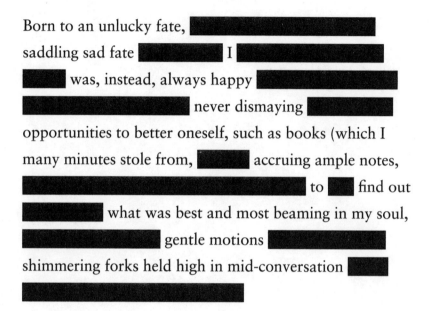

Born to an unlucky fate, ▮▮▮▮▮▮▮▮▮▮▮▮
saddling sad fate ▮▮▮▮▮▮ I ▮▮▮▮▮▮▮▮▮▮▮
▮▮▮▮ was, instead, always happy ▮▮▮▮▮▮▮▮
▮▮▮▮▮▮▮▮▮▮▮▮▮ never dismaying ▮▮▮▮▮▮
opportunities to better oneself, such as books (which I
many minutes stole from, ▮▮▮▮▮ accruing ample notes,
▮▮▮▮▮▮▮▮▮▮▮▮▮▮▮▮▮▮▮▮▮ to ▮▮ find out
▮▮▮▮▮▮ what was best and most beaming in my soul,
▮▮▮▮▮▮▮▮▮ gentle motions ▮▮▮▮▮▮▮▮▮
shimmering forks held high in mid-conversation ▮▮▮
▮▮▮▮▮▮▮▮▮▮▮▮▮▮

MICHELLE KENNEY & (ANTWON ROSE II)

████ my heart ██████

██████████ of such great exhaustion ██

only my deep

love for ██ you ██████████ after ██████

such Unholy slaughter ████████ must ████████

████████████ make it through ████████

████████████████████████████████

████████ I ████ cry. ████████████████

████████████ upon his Face upon the Ground. █

████████████ we would avenge even if it meant

stepping through the very gates of Hell.

DAUNTE WRIGHT

████████████ In my thrashing panic I have upended
████████ The blood, channeled within the floorboard
████████ pools ██████████████ the ████████ rug.
█████████████████ Who has not made a mistake? The
world is kind, it forgives, it is full of second chances. When
██
████ When █████████████████████████████████
████████████████

JUSTIFIED HOMICIDE

We are sorry, ███████ Sorry that we did not do more
████████

      ████████ when you still had the chance.
    We were afraid, █████████ Afraid for ourselves.
    ████████ Anxious █████████ in our
endeavor.
    ████████████████████
██

    We are sorry this happened ████████
    You did not deserve it, Mr. █████ said.
    And sorry, especially, that we did not stay ████████
██ as you
    went down, █████
    ████████████ said one of the hogs.

31

AIYANA JONES, AGE 7

██████ such love ████████████ such anticipation that
all that is
    lovely in life will be known by them, ████████████
███
███████████████████████████
    ████████████████████████████████████
the smell of
    the hair ████████ the feel of the tiny hand in yours—
and then the little
    one is gone! Taken! █████████████████████ such a
brutal violation ██
    ████████ in what had previously seemed a benevolent
world. ███████████████████████████ now, █
████████████ that love, ██████████████████████
the most abysmal suffering ████████

LAQUAN McDONALD

Did the thing merit ███████ the killing. ████████████
it was a technicality ████████ but ███ deeper, it was
something more. ██████████████████████████
███████████████ the boy he had been ███████████
███
standing in town ████████████████████████████
███
feeling strange and odd ████████████████████████
███
██████████████████████████ but also thinking,
quietly, there inside himself, that he might someday get
something for himself. And then, ████████████████
███
████████ bumbling █████████████████████████
███████████████████████ and ██████████████
wild ███████████████ nearly mad with ████████
███
██████████████████████████ some ████████████
████████████ language barely English

35

WHITE WITNESSES

As always at Sun's rising, 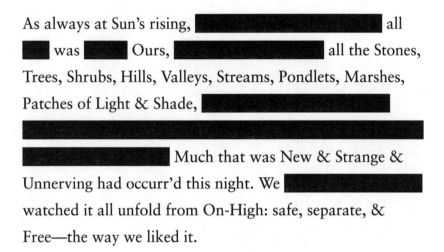 all
███ was ████ Ours, ███████████ all the Stones,
Trees, Shrubs, Hills, Valleys, Streams, Pondlets, Marshes,
Patches of Light & Shade, ████████████████
████████████████████████████████████
████████████████ Much that was New & Strange &
Unnerving had occurr'd this night. We ████████████
watched it all unfold from On-High: safe, separate, &
Free—the way we liked it.

BLACK WITNESS

From ▮▮▮ my left came a shout—of terror ▮▮▮▮▮

▮▮▮▮▮▮▮▮▮▮▮▮▮▮▮▮▮▮▮▮▮▮▮▮▮▮ always bone-

chilling, firesound ▮▮▮▮▮▮▮▮▮▮▮▮▮▮▮

▮▮▮▮▮▮▮

    Who had gone?

    I could not tell.

    And was still too under siege myself to care.

RODNEY KING

He was an open book. ▮▮▮▮▮▮▮▮▮▮▮▮▮▮▮▮▮▮
▮▮▮ opened up somewhat wider. By sorrow. ▮▮▮▮▮
By all of us, black and white, ▮▮▮▮▮▮▮▮▮▮▮▮
▮▮▮▮▮▮▮▮▮▮▮▮▮▮▮▮▮▮▮▮▮▮▮▮▮▮▮▮▮
▮▮▮▮▮▮▮▮▮▮▮▮ It had made him sad. ▮▮▮▮▮▮
All of us, white and black, had made him sadder, with our
sadness. ▮▮▮▮▮▮▮▮▮▮▮▮▮▮▮▮▮▮▮▮▮▮▮▮
▮▮▮▮▮▮▮▮▮▮▮▮▮▮▮▮▮▮▮▮▮▮▮▮▮▮▮▮▮
▮▮▮▮▮▮▮▮▮▮▮▮▮▮▮▮▮▮▮▮▮▮▮▮▮▮▮▮▮
▮▮▮▮▮▮▮▮▮▮▮▮▮▮▮ I thought, then, as hard as I
could, ▮▮▮▮▮▮▮▮▮▮▮▮▮▮▮▮▮▮▮▮▮▮ of all I
had heard ▮▮▮▮▮▮▮▮▮▮▮▮▮▮▮▮▮▮ regarding
▮▮▮▮▮▮ troubles and degradations, and called to mind,
▮▮▮▮▮▮▮ others ▮▮▮▮▮▮▮ I had known and loved
▮▮▮▮▮▮▮▮▮▮▮▮▮▮▮▮▮▮▮▮▮▮▮▮▮▮▮▮▮
▮▮▮▮▮▮▮▮▮▮▮▮▮▮▮▮▮▮▮▮▮▮▮▮ and all
the things that they had endured, ▮▮▮▮▮▮▮▮▮▮▮
▮▮▮▮▮▮▮▮▮▮▮▮▮▮▮▮▮▮▮▮▮▮▮▮▮▮▮▮▮
▮▮▮▮▮▮▮▮▮▮▮▮▮▮▮▮▮ We are ready, ▮▮ are
angry, are capable, ▮▮▮▮▮▮▮ are coiled up so tight as to
be deadly, or holy: turn us loose, ▮▮ let us at it, let us show
what we can do.

CIVIL OBEDIENCE

We are here ███████████████ Our ability to
abide ███████████████████████████ our
strength, ███████████████████████████
███████████ our central purpose. We ███████ wish,
███████████████████████████ for the
███████████ blessing of our continued abiding. For we are
here, but for how long, ███████████████████
███████████

SANDRA BLAND

What was done to her was done ███████████ by
many. What was done to her ████████████ was █
resisted, ████████████ which resulted, ███████
in her being sent ███ to some far worse place, ███
█████████████████████████████████████
█████████████████████ What was done to her
███████████████████████████████████████
███████████████████████████████████████
██████████████ drove her to hateful speech,
███████████████████████████████ drove her to
this ██████ silence. What was done to her was done by
big men, small men, boss men, men ██████████████
███████████████████████████████████████
█████████████████ who happened to be passing, ███
███████████ who spilled ███████████
████████████████ her there ████████████ What was
done to her was done on ████████ schedule, like some sort
of sinister church-going; ██████████████████
was ████████████████████████████████
██████████ looming and sanctioned; what was done to her
was straightforward ███████████████████████
███████████████████████████████████████

45

██████████████████████ what █████████████████

███

██████ country men ████ would never have dreamed of
doing ████████ to a woman of their own race), ████████

███

██ she nothing more than a ██████████ wax figure; ███████

███

███

███████████████████████ it could be done, ████████ it
was done, ██████ done ████████████

JAYLAND WALKER

publicly posted, an event that caused a great shock ▮▮▮
▮▮▮▮▮▮▮▮▮▮▮▮▮▮▮▮▮▮▮▮ unprecedented
thus far.

The details ▮▮▮▮▮▮▮▮▮▮▮▮▮▮▮▮
▮▮▮▮▮▮▮▮▮▮▮▮▮▮▮▮▮▮▮▮▮
▮▮▮▮▮▮▮▮▮▮▮▮▮▮▮▮▮▮
▮▮▮▮▮▮ that number ▮▮▮▮▮▮▮▮
▮▮▮▮▮ a ▮▮▮▮▮▮▮▮▮▮▮▮▮▮▮
devastating ▮▮▮▮▮▮▮▮▮▮▮▮
▮▮▮▮▮▮▮▮▮▮▮▮▮▮▮▮▮▮▮▮▮
▮ eighty-five ▮▮▮▮▮▮▮▮▮▮
▮▮▮▮▮▮▮▮▮ sweet Jesus. ▮▮▮▮▮
▮ threshed ▮▮▮▮▮▮▮▮▮▮▮▮▮
▮▮▮▮▮▮▮▮▮▮▮▮▮▮▮ Lord ▮▮▮
▮▮ that, ▮▮▮▮▮
▮▮▮▮▮ dead. That was something new. It seemed a
real war now.

MR. POLITICIAN

And I thought, then, as hard, as I could, ██████████
██████████
████████ of all I had heard ████████████████
████████ regarding ████████ troubles ████████████
██
██
██
████████████ and all the things ████████ endured,
████████ Sir, if you are as powerful as I feel that you are,
and as inclined toward us as you seem to be, endeavor to
do something for us, ████████████████████████████
████████ We are ████████ angry, ████████ our
hopes ████████████████████ dead ████████████
████████████████████████████████████

IN MEMORIAM

Trayvon Martin Mural

Katie Yamasaki

Michael Brown Mural

Will Kasso Condry

Tamir Rice Memorial

Photograph by Redux Picture

BLM Wall Mural

Renda Writer

Freddie Gray Mural

 Nether

.

Philando Castile Memorial

Photograph by Stephen Maturen, Getty Images

"History" Mural

Kyle Holbrook

Antwon Rose II Memorial

Photograph by Bill O'Toole

Elijah McClain

Thomas "Detour" Evans

Breonna Taylor Mural

Photograph by Maurice Taylor for Artists
and Volunteers, Annapolis, MD, Future History Now

Daunte Wright Memorial

Photograph by David Ryder

BLM Mural

Kyle Holbrook

Oscar Grant Mural

Refa One

Revolutionaries Mural

Jorit

Black Lives Matter Plaza

Commissioned by Mayor Muriel Bowser of
Washington, DC. Photograph by Anthony Tilghman

PART
TWO

PART
ONE

THE DILEMMA WE ALL LIVE WITH

I called ███████████████████████████████
███
███████████████████████████████████ we

were in a desperate situation ████████████████████
███

████████████████████

    How exactly would we say it? ████████████████
    We aren't exactly "kings of words"! ████████████
██

██████████████

    ██████████████████████ the architect of this place
has, for reasons we
    cannot know, deemed that ████████████████ to love
one's life enough to
    desire to stay here ██████████ a terrible sin, worthy
of the most severe punishment.
    Tell them we are tired of being nothing, and doing
nothing, and mattering not at all to anyone, and living in a
state of constant fear ████████████████

Not sure we can remember all that, said Mr. █████
    Sounds like quite a commitment, said Mr. █████

AHMAUD ARBERY

Jogging down the far side ██████████████ greeted
██████████ by a bull ████ looking forward ████
██████████████████████████████████
████████████████ might be ██████████
████ might reverse ████████████████████
████ might no longer ████████████████████
████ be ████████████████████████████ bouquet
of flowers, ████████████ once again ████████████
████████████

████ fire with no possible cause, as ████████ always
meticulously ████████
████████████████████████████████████
████████████ contentedly ████████████████████
████████████████████ anticipating ████████████
████████████

GEORGE FLOYD

All ██ quiet, dear Brother—Only the fire ████████

████

████████████████ where ████████

████████████████████████████

The moonlight shows the premises ████████

far & wide ████████████████████

████████████████████████████████ You

may recall a certain ████████ man ████████

████████████████████████ with one foot

on the neck ████████████ a certain mischievous

████ fellow threw ████ up there ████ until

████████████ the end ████████

████ no more—████

████████████████████████

████████ all, ████████████

████████████████████████████

████████████████ shaken by this proof of ██

mortality, stands a bit askew ████████

PROTEST SONG

████████████████████ now ████ mourners came ██ Hands extended. Sons intact. Wearing ██ their ████████████ sadness-masks ████████████████████████████████ ███████████████████ not ████████ alive ████████ ████ with ████████████ happiness at the potential of their still-living ████████████ I was ████ them. Strolling whistling ████████████████████████████████ ████████████████ able to ████████ dream and hope because it had not yet happened to me.

To us.

Trap. Horrible trap. At one's birth ████████████ Some last day must arrive. When you will need to get out of this body. ████████████████████████████████ ████████████████████████████████ All pleasures ████████ tainted by that knowledge. ██ ████ dear us ████████

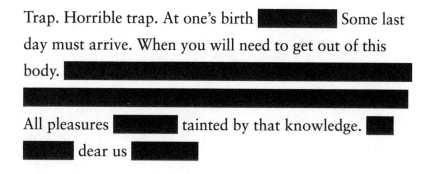

CURFEW HOUR

████████████████████████ tempted ██████ out ████████

████████████████████████████████ terrible judgment ████

you, ██████ say. Staying here, ████████████████ You

are dead, ████████████████████████████████████

████████████████ you must return █ your bodies, ████████

████████████████████████████ Do you really believe

██

██ you

shall ████ be allowed to linger here forever. ████████████

████████ in rebellion ████████████████████████

████████████████████ go.

WALTER SCOTT

And Lord the fellow ████████

████████ attempting to formulate a goodbye, in some sort

████████████████ not wishing to enact that final departure

in gloom, ███

██████████████████████████ was now ███████████████████

███████████████ sadness, ██████ and regret, ████████████

████████████████ he lingered, hoping for some comfort ██

████████████████ upon which he might expand.

████ nothing came.

██ he

directed his mind

outward, seeking the comfort of his life out there, and

the encouragement of his future, prospects, ████████████

████████████████████████████

no comfort was forthcoming, ████████████████████████

████ not, ██

████ anything at all.

ANDREW BROWN, JR.

And yet I knew with all my heart that ████████████
████████ We were at war. We were ██ at war. All was
chaos. All ██
communication. ████████████████████████████████
████████████ was mad. And yet I had seen it ████████████
could hear, in my mind, the sound it made as it functioned.

████████████████████

My God!

THE BLOODSHED

We black folks had ███████████ the church ████████
█████ Our experience having been that white people are
not especially fond of █████ us ████████████████████
██
███
█████
██
██
███████████████████████ killing must go hard against the will
of God. Where might God stand on this. He has shown us.
He could stop it. But has not. ████████████████████
████████████████████████████████ great beast
beyond our understanding, who ████████████████████
████████████████████████████████ is the spirit █
██████████████ and the ultimate end █████████████████
██
█████████████████ blood, more blood, ████████████
██████████ what ██████████████████████ should be.
██████████████████████ I do not know, and patiently wait
to learn, ███████████████████████████████████████
██████████████████████ anxiously, asking, What end ██████
██

101

SAMUEL DuBOSE

rode along ████████████████████████████ through
those quiet streets, ████████ not unhappy. ████████

██

██

████████████ Though ████████████████████████

████████ Anything could happen. ████████████ He
had forgotten. ████████████████ about the ████

████

████████████████████████

████████████████████ much ████████ He did ████████
to live. ████████████████████████████ There was so
much to do, ████████████████████████████████████
████████████████████████ in time (he told himself) it
would get better, and might even be good again. ████████

████████████████ It was hard. ████ for him. ████████

██

██

██

Tonight ████████████████████████████████████
████ slipped through him, into ████████████████████
that moment, ████████████████████████████████

██

 into the night, past the sleeping houses

SEAN BELL

Early in my youth ███████████████████████

██

██

██

██████████████████████████████

█████████████████████████████████████ marry,

██████████████████████████████████████

████████ I wished to ████████ (as I believe all wish

to be happy), ████████████████████████

██

████████████████████████ no hope for us, ████████

███████████████████████ stops-and-starts, and fresh

beginnings, and heartfelt resolutions, ████████████

██

██████████████ one afternoon, ████████████████

██

██

████████████████████████████████ I ████████████

████████ depart ███████████████████ rather savagely

████████████████████

████████ nauseous at the quantity of blood ████████████

 I settle

woozily　　　　　　　　 at which time

I realize how unspeakably beautiful all of this was,

the gift of being allowed, every day, to wander this vast　　　 paradise,

109

DEAR MR. LEGISLATOR

The ████████████████████████ poured out, ██████
██ sons, brothers, husbands ████████████████████
██████ ever realize that ██ desolation, sorrow, grief ██
pervades this country ██████████████ that the young
men who have been ██████████████ murdered, ██████
██████████████ owe it to your ████████ irresolution &
want of moral courage?

PHILANDO CASTILE

▮▮▮▮ as is often ▮▮▮▮▮ my hopes were ▮▮▮▮▮▮▮▮▮
▮▮▮▮▮▮▮▮▮▮▮▮▮▮▮▮▮▮▮▮▮▮▮▮ not generous.
He was ▮▮▮▮▮▮▮▮ rough with me ▮▮▮▮▮
▮▮▮▮▮▮▮▮▮▮▮▮▮▮▮▮▮▮▮▮▮▮▮▮▮▮▮▮▮
▮▮▮▮▮▮▮▮▮▮▮▮▮▮▮▮▮▮▮▮▮▮▮▮▮▮▮▮▮

▮▮▮▮▮▮▮▮▮ He did not seem to see me, but only
endeavored to possess me; ▮▮▮▮▮▮▮▮▮▮▮▮
▮▮▮▮▮▮▮▮▮▮▮▮▮▮▮▮▮▮▮▮▮▮▮▮▮▮▮▮▮
▮▮▮▮▮▮▮▮▮▮▮▮▮▮▮▮▮▮▮▮▮ I ▮▮ had
truth and value ▮▮▮▮▮▮▮▮▮▮▮▮▮▮▮▮▮▮
▮▮▮▮▮▮▮▮▮▮▮▮▮ he ▮▮▮▮▮▮▮▮▮▮▮▮▮
▮▮▮▮▮▮▮▮▮▮▮▮▮▮▮▮▮▮▮▮▮▮▮▮▮▮▮
finding himself thus disrespected, ▮▮▮▮▮▮▮▮
▮▮▮▮▮▮▮▮▮▮▮▮▮▮▮▮▮▮▮▮▮▮▮▮▮▮▮▮▮
▮▮▮▮▮▮▮▮▮▮▮▮▮▮▮▮▮▮▮▮▮▮▮▮▮▮▮▮▮
▮▮▮▮▮▮▮▮▮▮
    that was that. ▮▮▮▮▮▮▮▮▮▮▮▮▮▮▮▮▮
▮▮▮▮▮▮▮▮▮▮▮ he ▮▮▮▮▮▮▮▮ some minor
functionary ▮▮▮▮▮▮▮▮▮▮▮▮▮▮▮▮▮▮▮▮
▮▮▮▮▮▮▮▮▮▮▮▮▮▮▮▮▮▮▮▮▮▮▮▮▮▮▮▮▮
▮▮▮▮▮▮▮▮▮▮▮▮▮▮▮▮▮▮▮▮▮▮▮▮▮▮▮▮▮
pompous little nobody ▮▮▮▮▮▮▮ I had been ▮▮

beautiful ███████████████████████████
████████ in ██ heart, ████████ not ██████████
██████████████ "an inferior species," █████████████
And then, ███████████ to have him shoot me ████████
██
██
███████████████████ it ██████████████████████
██
██████████████████████████████ was

more than I could bear.

LEVAR JONES

██████████████████████

You will ████ sir, please, remain calm, ██████ We have no enmity

between us of which I am aware. Let us regard this ████ simple business ████████ I will hand you my wallet, just so, and then, ██████████████████████

No, no, no.

No no no.

Entirely the wrong & illogical thing for you ██

██████████████████████

██ I am punctured.

BREONNA TAYLOR

███████████████████████████ Tremors ran through
her body. Her form flickered ██████████████████
████████████ in ██████████ place ████████████
████████████████ shameful to mention ████████████
the ██████ future ████ she had, ███████████████
████████████ attentive mother; ████████ baker of bread
and cakes; ██████ church-attender; respected ████████
██████████████████████████████ adoring, █████████████

HEREAFTER

███████████████████████████████

And Mother? ██████ Please know. ██████████
██████ You did the best you could. We blame you for
nothing. ████████████████████████████████████
████████████████████████████████
████████████████████████████

Whatever failures you feel ███████████████████
██████████████ leave them behind ███████████ All
turned out beautifully. █████████████
██████████████████ I ████████████
███████ a wave ██████ crashed upon the shore, ███
███

███████████████████████
█████████████████████ racing back.
██████████████
███
████████████████████████████
███████████████████
████████████████ Watch this.

STEPHON CLARK

██████████████████████████████████ I moved past
Flower-bright Hedges in the full Flush of my Youth, ███
████████████████ All who
    saw, █████████████████████████████
████████████
      ████████████████████ would step aside, awed, ███
███
██
██ in the
Night ██████████ pounding ███████████████
██████████ pounding ████████████████████
███████████████████ indeed, dark as Night, ███████
██
   ████████████████████████████ & Ignoring
the Cries
    ██████████████████████████

FREDDIE GRAY

████████████████████████████ did
away with ██████████████████████████
██████████████████████████████████
██████████████████████████████
(his) ████████████████ natural expression
of ██ love ██████████████
██████████████████████ and ██████████
██████████ time ████████████████████
██████████████████████████████████
███████████ to be more ████████████ in
the world, ██████████████████████████
██████████████████████████████████
██████████ his ██████████████████████ total
happiness.

SAMARIA RICE & (TAMIR RICE)

████████████████████████

I was in error ███████████████████████████████ thought
I would have him forever. He was ██████████████████ but
always just a passing, temporary energy-burst. ████████████
██
██

██ had never stayed the same, even instant to instant.
He came out of nothingness, took form, was loved, ████
████████████████████████████████

Only I did not think it would be so soon.
Or that he would precede us.
██
████████████████████████████████

I mistook him for a solidity, and now ██████████
██
██ the greater
city not stable and the wide world not stable. All ████ are
altering, in every instant.
████████████████████
███
██████████

ELIJAH McCLAIN

█████████████████████████ so unfair. █████████████
so keenly discriminating. ██████████████████████████
████████ I believe you would have recognized me for the
great ████ I was. If only ███████████████████████████
███
████ You could have ████████████████████ seen ████
██████████████████████████ from the heart, ████
acknowledging that I was ████████████████████████
███
███████████ the finest █████ of my generation.

GENERATIONS (AN ELEGY)

██████████████████ inclined toward sorrow; toward
the fact that the world was full of sorrow; █████████
███████████████████
  █████████████████████████████████
████████████████
  ██████████████████████████████████ (none
content; █
    wronged, neglected, overlooked, misunderstood), ████
███████████
  █████████████████████████████████████
█████████████████
  ████████████████ his current state of sorrow was not
uniquely his, █████████
█ but, ██████████████ had been felt, would yet be felt,
by scores of others, in all times, ██████████████████
████████████████████████████████ in this state, he
could be ███████████ to anyone ████████████████████
███████████████████████████ of great help or great
harm, ███████████████████████████████

131

BOTHAM JEAN

███████████████████████████████████

███████████████████ brighten ████████████████

███████████████████████████████████

███████████████ in ways I cannot adequately explain. I
had been happy, happy enough, ███████████████
████ uttering a spontaneous prayer that went, simply:
████ here, still here. ███████████ a rushing river ██████

███████████████████████████████████

████████████ and the awareness of something ██████

███████████████████████████ moving ████████████
one evening, unprompted, ███████████████████

█████████████████████ I was a good man: thoughtful,
intelligent, kind.

ALL OUR SINS

Whatever my sin, it must, I felt ███████ be small,
compared to the sins of these. And yet, ██████████████
Was I not? ████████████████████████████ to ███
them
 ██████████████████████████████████ fearsome
██
██████████████████ but as lamb ████████████████
██████ with neither affection nor malice; ████████████
██████ while others are released to the meadow, ██████
██████ according to a standard we are too lowly to discern.
 It is only for us to accept; ██████████ judgment, and our
punishment. ████████████████ this teaching ████████
██████

 ██████████ sick, sick at heart.

END RACISM

IN CONVERSATION: GEORGE SAUNDERS AND CRYSTAL SIMONE SMITH

CRYSTAL: I was reading your novel when the BLM protests were happening, and the idea of lost souls in a "bardo" state really spoke to me. I suspect many readers are not familiar with this term, "bardo." Can you explain what it is?

GEORGE: Sure. "Bardo" is a term from Tibetan Buddhism that basically means "transitional state." There are many bardos, but the term is often used to refer to the space between death and the next rebirth. In the context of the book, both Lincolns, Abe and Willie, are in transition; Willie has just died and Lincoln is trying to transition out of his grief and back into the world.

CRYSTAL: I think the bardo state was a very compelling motif. While reading your novel, I was deeply drawn to the disturbed, grief-stricken dead characters, or spirits, rather. I had parallel thoughts about the many young Black souls who are killed and left in a similar state—their lives taken unjustly and violently—how they become public tragedies. I wondered what they might say if they too could speak from the grave about their deaths. That's how many of the poems dedicated to the victims originated.

GEORGE: I was really moved that you chose my text to generate your erasure poems. The result is so beautiful and moving. Thank you for doing it. Was there a particular passage that first prompted your creative response?

CRYSTAL: The BLM movement was in its third day of protests after George Floyd's death. I was pretty distraught, so I sat skimming the chapters more so than reading. I arrived at chapter 78, in which the character, roger bevins iii, summons others to assist him in saving Willie from the Bardo. There were eerie moments in the passage, like "*we are tired of being nothing, and doing nothing, and mattering not at all to anyone,*" that mirrored reality at the time. It was here certain words began to illuminate the pages, becoming a poem and new narrative.

GEORGE: In my book, Lincoln is consumed with grief at the death of his eleven-year-old son, Willie. Why do you think it is that so many Americans fail to empathize with that same grief and sense of loss when a young member of a Black family is killed?

CRYSTAL: We are all humans, yet our racial and class differences don't always allow us to see ourselves in one another. Unspeakable atrocities happen in our communities because, too often, human life is distinguished along the lines of race and social status. These problematic distinctions lay the groundwork for violence against Black lives. Some Americans have a hard time recognizing the worth and dignity of every person.

GEORGE: Yes. That's one thing I love about writing fiction or poetry: the way it gives the writer a chance to cut past the superficial ornamentations of class and race and gender and all of that and recognize that suffering is suffering. I think one of the ongoing curses of our historical racism and segregation in daily life is that it allows for a lot of empty projection; white people imagining Black lives in a certain way, absent of the grounding in the actual that would engender compassion and sympathy. I think that's one of the real gifts your book offers the reader: It helps us really feel the preciousness of the lives being lost, and the palpable reality of the sorrow associated with being a parent having to feel worried about the safety of one's children for no other reason than the color of their skin.

CRYSTAL: I didn't realize, when I first created the poems derived from the text of your novel, that it would create a long legal process seeking permission to use your words. I will always appreciate the fact that you supported *Dark Testament*. You didn't have to, so why did you choose to get involved?

GEORGE: Really, I just felt a deep sense of wanting to support a fellow artist who had done something so wonderful that seemed to be coming right from her heart.

CRYSTAL: You teach creative writing at Syracuse University. Is there a piece of advice you can give readers who hope to write themselves?

GEORGE: Well, it sounds so simple, but I really do subscribe to "Writing is rewriting." There's something really liberating about knowing that we don't have to "get it right" in the first draft and, in fact, that nobody gets it right that early. For me, writing is a process of trying to revise the falseness and manipulation out of the prose and, by association, out of myself. In my experience, that's the difference between a good writer and a, you know, published one: the ability to go back into a text in a good, playful spirit, and improve it.

CRYSTAL: I agree 100 percent that rewriting is the key to writing well. Also, I don't think successful writers write fearlessly. For me, it is the process of making notes about what you think and being willing to go to uncomfortable places. I write about things I fear and things I find disturbing, with the goal of taking those personal thoughts or stories to a greater, universal audience.

ACKNOWLEDGMENTS

I am grateful to the Poetry Foundation and *POETRY* magazine for publishing and featuring the following poems: "Rodney King," "Oscar Grant," and "Black Mothers and Sons."

To Liz Nealon and the team at Great Dog Literary, thank you for giving me an audience and for your extraordinary belief in this book.

To Kate Farrell at Henry Holt Books for Young Readers, thank you for ushering this book into a young and hope-filled world. Thank you also to Linda Minton, copyeditor, and Taylor Pitts, proofreader.

To George Saunders, whose novel *Lincoln in the Bardo* made these poems possible. Your immense talent is matched only by your immense heart. Thank you for your support and encouragement. I walk in a space of gratitude.

Grateful acknowledgment to members of the Carolina African American Writers Collective and to the many writers who inspire me to carry on. You are my well-wishers, counselors, and advocates. I am lucky.

Special gratitude to early supporters of this book: Haven

Kimmel Holmes, C. P. Mangel, Reginald Dwayne Betts, Tony Medina, and Carole Boston Weatherford.

> *History, despite its wrenching pain,*
> *Cannot be unlived, but if faced*
> *With courage, need not be lived again.*
> —Maya Angelou, "On the Pulse of Morning"

To the Black Lives Matter movement, your acts of courage while under siege humble me beyond words. Thank you for your voices and devotion to justice.

To Cameron and Sidney, whom I was blessed to birth, survival is no light work. Go well. Learn to love what's beautiful about life, and to face, bravely, what's difficult.

To Maury, whose steady presence and love make this life possible.

> *I have been enslaved, yet my spirit is unbound.*
> *I have been cast aside, but I sparkle in the darkness.*
> *I have been slain but live on in the river of history.*
> —Pauli Murray, from "Prophet," *Dark Testament*

The title of this book, *Dark Testament*, was adopted from Pauli Murray's only collection of poems, first published in 1970. Her testimonial poems reflect the brutal history of slavery, the Jim Crow era, and the unfinished dream of racial justice.

ABOUT THE ARTISTS

THOMAS EVANS, aka **Detour**, is an all-around creative specializing in large-scale public art, interactive visuals, portraiture, immersive spaces, and creative directing. His focus is to create work where art and innovation meet. Detour's murals occupy the space at the intersection of contemporary art and community. They seek to highlight the heart and soul of their surroundings and provide a unique visual representation of many authentic community members, many of whom have never had their likeness incorporated into any form of art. With each mural, there is a relationship-building opportunity, which results in a product that is derived from the community.

GAIA grew up in New York City and is a graduate of the Maryland Institute College of Art. His studio work, installations, and gallery projects have been exhibited throughout the world, most notably at the Baltimore Museum of Art, the Rice Gallery in Houston, the Palazzo Collicola Arti Visive in Spoleto, and the Civil and Human Rights Museum in Atlanta. His street work has been documented and featured in several books on urban art, including *Beyond the Street: The 100 Leading Figures in Urban Art* (Berlin, 2010) and *Outdoor Gallery: New York City* (New York, 2014).

Gaia lives and works in Baltimore, Maryland, but spends a majority of his time painting murals across the world. He has produced works in all six habitable continents.

KYLE HOLBROOK is an American digital artist, graphic designer, muralist, author, and filmmaker. He grew up drawing almost all the time, handcrafting holiday and birthday cards that became sought-after treasures. His parents—teachers in the Pittsburgh and Steel Valley school districts—encouraged his efforts and exposed him to new vistas: an uncle's farm near Ithaca, New York; a Native American reservation outside of Taos, New Mexico; a summer-long sojourn with his father, an amateur photographer, capturing images across forty states. Kyle studied at the Art Institute of Pittsburgh, designing T-shirts and clothing in his spare time. Gangs were an influence in his teenage years, but Holbrook never missed his Saturday art classes at Carnegie Mellon University. After becoming a father, Holbrook started KH Design studio at the age of nineteen.

NETHER is a globally traveled street artist with an extensive body of public works spanning his native city of Baltimore, Maryland. Nether's work is a social and cultural documentarian of the struggles, histories, aspirations, and dilemmas that our cities face. Many of his works are created in the spirit of guerilla beautification, and they are sometimes strategically positioned to spark conversations on ignored urban issues. Woven into the works is a spiritual sense of balance and design aimed at evoking an understanding of our relationship with our surrounding environments and the places we call home. Outdoor works are often designed with guidance from or in conceptual collaboration with stakeholders. The quest can be seen as an attempt to help refuel and engage the landscape, bring out the city's pride, and capture the poetic chaos that defines BMORE.

JOSEPH RENDA JR. is a Chicago-based artist whose paintings capture the inherent connection humans have with the natural world. His work is highly realistic, bringing detailed depictions to life by juxtaposing them with surrealistic imagery. He urges his audience to surrender to nature's pull and connect with their roots while viewing his paintings. Renda earned a bachelor of fine arts specializing in oil painting from the American Academy of Art.

KEISHA FINNIE was born and raised in Lancaster, Pennsylvania. Her inspiration comes from simply living life and being a woman of color. She uses her art to express her thoughts and feelings around self-identity. Being Black is a big part of that, because the world never forgets to remind her. Her art comes from a combination of her love for nature, vibrant color, texture, and the female form. It's a reflection of herself while connecting the viewer to her perspective of the world.

REFA ONE, a native of Oakland, California, has for over two decades been instrumental in the development of the innovative, unorthodox genre of art known as Aerosol Art (graffiti art/style writing). Immersed in hip-hop culture as a youth, he used the walls of urban structures as his canvas. Refa's refined hip-hop calligraphy speaks to a legacy of style writing, a cultural tradition born from the New York City subway painting movement.

WILL KASSO CONDRY is a renowned visual artist, graffiti scholar, and educator living in Vermont. Growing up in the inner city of Trenton, New Jersey, Kasso's only escape from the negative images that plagued his community was art. Painting and drawing became his loyal friends at a time when many of his peers were falling victim to the streets.

JORIT, who was born in Italy, started spray painting at the age of thirteen. For him, writing on the city walls was a way to escape from a world that was oppressive and not stimulating. Known for his hyperrealistic mural portraits, Jorit's aim is for his art to reflect his reality. He finds faces are the most telling because they indicate someone's emotions so directly. This interest in the varied incarnations of the human countenance has prompted him to craft candid portraits all the way from the rural stretches of Cuba to New York City.